"[Long] is succeeding in taking a concept and really developing it into something new, making it his own ... his works could grow into a hit."
—DAVE FARLAND, Runelords

OF ICE & MAGIC

Hugh B. Long

Printed in the United States of America

First Printing: Jul 2015

Typeset in Garamond 11pt

Published by: Asgard Studios
Ottawa, Canada
www.asgard-studios.com

ISBN: 978-1927646595

Library and Archives Canada Cataloguing in Publication

Pending

Chapter One

THE OLD GODS DIED. MAGIC died. I wept to see them gone.

I had been born in a world overflowing with magic and gods, in a time when bravery was the most noble of virtues and a maiden the most treasured prize. Such is not the state of the world today.

While I relax on a bed of velvet, safe behind glass walls which stand upon a finely crafted oak floor, people come to admire my beauty. They glimpse their faces in the reflection of my perfect skin and marvel at the lines and curves of my exquisite physical form.

True, I bask in their admiration, and their envy that they are not as well formed. Yet my home is but a prison.

I have lived, or should I say, existed, for a thousand years. I say that because living implies freedom and I have none. As the lights fade each night and my admirers retire, I slip into a world of dreams, a world filled with my past glories.

It began at the ends of the world, on an island of ice and magic which had risen up from the frigid sea. On that island a clever smith named Fornulf had built a forge into the side of a great fiery mountain. Not an ordinary forge, mind you, it was a fjor'tyna—a life-forge.

Certainly he could make common weapons there; they were the building blocks of his marvelous works, but a life forge was a womb that birthed the most marvelous of artifacts. The most cherished of these were the fjor-sverds—the living swords. Some said Fornulf had studied under the ancient dwarven smiths, the sons of Ivaldi, but who can say.

Fornulf was an apt name for him as it meant ancient wolf. With his graying hair and silver beard he looked the part. He was cunning too. And I do not mean just in ways of smithing. No, he was too clever by half for any mortal man, though he spoke little, causing many to underestimate his guile. I warn you now, never underestimate a life forger; for only the wisest and most cunning of men can learn such art.

Under a full moon, Fornulf's forge glowed with a hellish hue as the bellows sprayed water to cool the magma, great clouds of searing steam exploding into the air. This was no ordinary forge. Here on the edge of the ancient mountain, raging fire and horrendous heat were ever present as molten rock flowed from the depths of Muspelheim, the kingdom of Surt and home of the fire giants. While a normal forge must be stoked to breathe life into it, the life-forge had to be cooled, so water was pumped over the lava to regulate the heat.

Hues of sunset and blood illuminated the small stone room. Fornulf's heavy leather apron hung singed and burned from a thousand such nights at the forge. The leathery skin on his arms and face was in no better shape.

On that moonlit night, Fornulf's hammer rang against a blade as it struck the anvil. Sparks flew and the sword blade sang at its makers bidding. Fornulf's son, Karl, had been his apprentice for six seasons. He was handsome and strong, and almost a man at seventeen years old.

Karl held the sword on the anvil with a pair of tongs, flipping it as his father struck the blade. Every so often Fornulf would thrust the blade back into the maw of the life-forge allowing the liquid rock to sear the metal. Karl would pump the bellows, causing the lava to scream as the water cooled its brilliant skin to black. Then the hammering and flipping would continue.

The blade had been forged of sky-iron, taken from a rock that fell from the sky. Such metal was said to have much magic.

3

To that twisted lump, Fornulf added ores of gold and silver, and one thing rarer than all: powdered diamond. A life-forged blade was the most expensive weapon a noble could buy; no commoner could ever afford one.

Fornulf had come from the northern mainland, but now made his home on the island of ice and fire. He'd brought his new bride and their two babes to make a fresh start after a plague had taken his first wife and four of their children. He`d married again, in his mid thirties, but he was an old man now—fifty-one winters he'd seen.

Fornulf delivered one last hammer blow to the blade, then held it up to his eyes for inspection, scanning the yard-long length of fine steel, admiring the herringbone pattern and the runes incised on the blade. He nodded, satisfied with his work, then thrust the full length of the steel into a barrel of rendered whale oil to temper the blade. This was the most critical part of the process. The oil hissed, popped and bubbled as the metal cooled.

He motioned to Karl who immediately went out, returning a short time later with a naked young man, perhaps eighteen, followed by an older man in dark grey robes.

"Are you ready?" Fornulf ask the naked youth. The young man nodded, shivering in the cold air, protecting his modesty with his hands.

No names were exchanged. True names held great power

over the owner of them. When magical forces were called upon, as they were about to be, every precaution was taken. The older man in the grey robes was simply known as a vitki—a wise man. He was skilled in the way of galdr magic, the spells of which were chanted.

A middle aged woman in a green robe slipped into the room as well. She was a seithkona—a spirit walker. She carried with her a hide covered drum.

Karl ushered the naked man to a stout oak table, where he was instructed to lay down. Fornulf carried the now cold sword blade in his bare hands.

"You must take the blade and hold it against your body. Do you understand?" Fornulf asked him.

The naked man nodded nervously.

"You do this of your own free will?" Fornulf asked him.

The naked man nodded again.

"I need you to say the words aloud so that the gods may hear you," Fornulf said.

"I do this of my own free will and offer my life force to the sword," the naked man said evenly.

Fornulf nodded to the vitki and the seithkona. Aside from Fornulf, they were the only two practitioners of the elder arts on the island, so rare were their gifts.

From inside his robes, the vitki produced a wooden wand, carved intricately with runic patterns. He walked to one side of the table where the naked man lay, and began to chant. The seithkona did likewise, standing across from the vitki, joining the chant beating her drum rhythmically.

The nameless, naked man, held the sword across his chest and abdomen, trembling. Drumbeats and resonant chanting suffused the room. The ceremony may have lasted for minutes or hours, for time has no meaning when the worlds of men and gods touch, as they did that night.

The sword began to hum, to vibrate, to glow; the galdr chanting and drumbeats infused it with eldritch energy. The naked man began to vibrate . . . and to fade. At the perfect moment, Fornulf drew a dagger across the naked man's throat and blood flooded the table.

The blade burned brighter, and brighter, threatening to blind them all, and the naked man faded away, like morning mist under the light of the sun. Fornulf threw up an arm to shield his eyes from the glowing metal, but as quickly as the light had flared, it was gone. The vitki and seithkona fell silent and silence filled the room. No, not quite silence. There was something. The blade . . . whispered.

The *sacrifice* had been accepted.

The next day great shadows slithered against the backdrop of jagged mountains. Fornulf had stepped outside of his house and gazed up at them. The rock on the island was as black as ink, much darker than his native lands. The seasonal moss and lichen spattered the black canvas in patterns of greens and yellows. Fornulf's forge lay at the end of a deep canyon on the side of a fiery mountain, where liquid rock bubbled up from the bowls of the underworld.

"Riders," Karl said.

Fornulf brushed soot from his apron and tried to make himself presentable. He'd worked throughout the night, as he had to finish fitting the hilt and cross-guard for the sword. It was done now. The sword was polished and oiled, ready for its new master. His family were quick to line up in front of the house, anxious to meet the wealthy gothi, or chief, for the first time.

Six riders on well-bred horses galloped up the track to Fornulf's modest farmstead. Perched arrow-straight on the back of white stallion, sat Torgny Magnisson, Chief of Aegisheim. He'd been chief of the South Farthing for only a few years, taking over when his brother had died. It had been a bitter succession, as his brother had a son and heir. Torgny had judged the boy too young and had assumed the mantle of chief for himself. Of course, Torgny was the wealthiest man in the entire South Farthing, if not on the whole island, and few would dare to challenge him, lest they find their debts suddenly called in, or fail to find favor in days to come.

Fornulf's forge lay on the western edge of the Eastfjord Farthing, close enough to Torgny's territory, but he'd had few dealings with him till now. He'd made weapons and armor for Torgny's men, but had never crafted anything for the chief himself.

Clad in bright mail and backed by a fine blue cloak, Torgny slid from his stallion. He was balding, but wore a well-trimmed beard that had once been straw colored, but now hung streaked with grey.

Fornulf limped forward, an old injury acting up that morning. He gave a slight bow. "Lord, it is an honor to have you at our humble steading."

"Of course it is," Torgny said with a smug smile.

Fornulf hadn't expected that and felt rather uncomfortable.

"I jest, good smith, I jest!" Torgny said, clapping both hands on Fornulf's shoulders. "Thank you for welcoming me to your home." Suddenly Torgny's nose twitched and he recoiled, his face twisting in disgust. "Gods above, what is that smell? Rotten eggs?"

"Ah, apologies, Lord. Vapors from the depths of the earth. We have grown accustomed to it living here. Like the urine pits of the weavers, the vapors are our burden."

Torgny's face wriggled under the assault, but he seemed to master his disgust. "You're a brave man, Fornulf." He smiled.

"May I present my family, Lord?"

Torgny made a sweeping gesture. "By all means."

"This is my wife, Hildegund"

Torgny gave a nod to Hildegund and followed along with Fornulf's introductions.

"This strapping young man is my son, Karl."

Torgny gave him an appraising nod. "Strong. Good stock, eh?" he said looking at Fornulf. "He'll make a good warrior I'd wager."

Fornulf cleared this throat. "I hope he will make an even better fjorsmythr, Lord. He is my apprentice."

"Indeed, a much rarer resource," Torgny said.

"And this," Fornulf said, " is my daughter, Berengara."

Torgny's eyes grew wide at the sight of Berengara, and he said nothing for a moment. Fornulf's daughter had that affect on men, such was her beauty—so like her mother.

Seeing Torgny's discomfort and Berengara's, Fornulf spoke up. "I'll be looking for a husband for her this year, Lord. If you know of any good matches, I'd be much obliged for your counsel. She'll be sixteen in a couple of moons."

"Marriage?" Torgny said, trailing off. "Of course. Yes. She is … lovely." He seemed to shake himself out of his fugue. "I will see what I can do." He turned to Fornulf "Now, to business, good man. I believe you have something for me?"

"Yes, Lord." Fornulf motioned to Karl, who produced a clean sheepskin bundle. Fornulf took the bundle reverently and turned back to Torgny. He inclined his head and unwrapped the bundle.

Lying on the wool side of the sheepskin, the completed sword glistened. Its handle carved of walrus ivory, and inlaid with tiny sapphires. Inset silver wire wound around the ivory, and runes representing *hail* and *ice* lay boldly stamped on the cross guard and hilt of the blade.

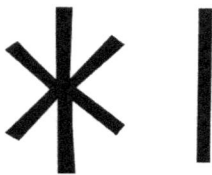

"You'll notice it's imbued with the runes for hail and ice, as you requested. As you use the sword, it's will and yours will become one, it's powers shaped by the union of your two life forces."

Torgny nodded absently.

"But what are these runes carved down the central groove of the blade?" Torgny asked.

ᚢᛚᚠᛒᛖᚱᚻᛏ

Fornulf smiled, nodding. "Those are runes for ULFBERHT. He is the fabled fjorsmythr, the first of us, and my own master. His school is one of legend, and there is only one apprentice at a time. Ulfberht is now dead, and I have assumed my master's fjorsmythr mantle. My son, Karl, is now the only living apprentice. Every sword that I forge bears Ulfberht's name to honor his memory and his gifts to mankind."

Torgny said nothing, he just stood, mouth agape.

"Have you a name for it, Lord?" Fornulf asked.

"Magnificent," Torgny whispered.

"Its name, Lord?"

Torgny shook his head, appearing bewitched for the second time today. "No- I mean, yes, I have a name for it. Isbrunna."

"Iceburn, that is a beautiful name, Lord."

Torgny motioned for the blade. "May I?"

Fornulf held out the blade. "Of course, Lord."

Torgny held the sword like a child with his first honeycomb. He was giddy with delight and Fornulf thought the Chief might actually cry. Torgny stepped back a few paces and swung the sword in a few arcs, marveling at the balance and lightness.

"It feels alive in the hand!" Torgny exclaimed.

"They do, Lord." And of course, that wasn't just metaphorically speaking—the swords had a soul, a will, if only a shadow of its former self. "Your sword's power will blossom as you use it. As you and the sword become accustomed to each other, your mastery of its power will grow. Like any new skill, Lord, it will take some getting use to."

"Have you made many?" Torgny asked, never taking his eye from Isbrunna.

"No, Lord. Only a handful these last thirty years. Only

nobles such as yourself have the silver to pay for the materials." What he didn't add, as the chief well knew, was the fact that such a blade demanded a living sacrifice—a *willing* sacrifice. A man had to pay a fortune for a someone to give his life willingly to a blade. Those who did might be down on their luck and were offered fortunes, or position for their family, in exchange for their sacrifice—a price very few wanted to pay. It did not mean offering their *lives*, it meant offering their *souls*. The sacrifice would then dwell inside that weapon until it was destroyed, or until the end of time itself.

"Well, then I count myself very lucky that you sailed to our little island, Fornulf."

"It pleases me to know my work will bless your household, Lord."

Torgny handed the sword back to Fornulf who wrapped it up in the sheepskin. Torgny snapped his fingers. "Kraka." A wiry man with a wild and frizzy head of red hair, and a matching beard, retrieved the bundle.

"Now, if only my leatherworker can craft a scabbard to do Isbrunna justice …" Torgny trailed off.

"Your man Sigurd is a fine craftsman, Lord, I know him well. You're lucky to retain him."

Torgny produced a pouch from beneath his blue cloak, handing it to Fornulf. "For your work, Fornulf."

He took the pouch and was surprised at its weight. It had to be much more than he was promised.

Torgny must have noticed Fornulf's surprise and said, "A little extra for you."

"Lord," Fornulf said bowing.

Torgny glanced back at Berengara again before he turned on his heel and mounted his white stallion. "Gods keep you well, Fornulf and family." Torgny waived and set his horse to a canter. His men quickly followed.

"What a lovely man," Hildegund said.

Fornulf opened the pouch, eyes wide. "And generous too," he said suspiciously as he considered the weight of the pouch in his hands, "this has to be twice what we agreed for my fee."

Chapter Two

THE NEXT MORNING FORNULF AWOKE, still weary from his labors at the life-forge the night before last. Creating such artifacts took concentration beyond most men, and it taxed him so. He sat down at the kitchen table beside his daughter, who was playing with an old sword of his. Despite her mother's lessons in weaving and naal binding, Berengara often practiced with Fornulf's sword and spear. She entertained fantasies of becoming a Valkyrie—one of the goddess Freya's holy shield-maidens who chose the slain on the battlefield. The chosen would then go to Valhalla. He smiled. She was his baby, and he liked to indulge her.

Hildegund had prepared a hearty breakfast of rye porridge

and eggs for them. Fornulf watched her, admiring her beauty, the fair hair and sea blue eyes. She was still so young—he was almost twenty-years her senior. He'd never looked at another women since he'd met Hildegund—well, unless he counted that minor dalliance with one of the old chief's serving maids, a Welsh slave girl named Idelle, but that had been almost fifteen years ago, just after they'd arrived on the island.

He and Hildegund had been blessed with two healthy, fine looking children; Karl their oldest, and their daughter, Berengara. Once again he pondered the need to find her a husband—she was almost sixteen, after all. Maybe Chief Torgny would find her a good match. A minor noble maybe?

Despite having everything he'd ever wanted within the walls of their modest house, this morning he felt hollow. Such was the weight of knowledge of what he'd just crafted. Men would kill each other, regardless of whether Fornulf walked the world or not, but as he grew older, he thought more about his part in things. Perhaps he felt regret. But once a man embarked on a long journey, starting over was almost impossible. His skills fed his loved ones, and that necessity outweighed his guilty conscience.

Hildegund bent down to kiss her husband's head as she passed him. "Why the dour look, husband?"

He looked up and kissed her chin as she shuffled away. "Oh, I'm fine. I'm taking the boy to town, Hild. We've supplies to fetch. Should be back in two or three days."

"I know," Hildegund said. "Karl told me this morning."

Berengara beamed, slamming the sword down on the table, toppling a cup of goat's milk. Her long brown hair fell around her face. "May I come? I'd like to go." She nodded enthusiastically, as if that would persuade him. "I could help," she added tentatively, ignoring the spreading pool of goat's milk on the table.

Fornulf knew exactly what his daughter wanted—a chance to gossip with the other girls in town. She'd get nothing done, and what's more, he'd have to hunt her down before they left, like as not.

"Not this time, Brynn." He'd given her the pet name, which meant mail-armor. He felt it reflected her oftentimes tough exterior. "Your mother needs help around the farm." He knew that wasn't entirely true—she could be spared for a few days. And he knew that she knew. Their farm was modest, only producing a few hardy vegetables, some meat from pigs and milk from the goats. His smithing provided most of the family's income.

But, he'd raised an obedient, though spirited, daughter. She knew better than to argue and just scowled at him, stomping a foot beneath the table. Gods above, she'd be a handful for her future husband. He almost smiled at the thought.

"Where's Karl?" he asked Hildegund.

"Already up, out, and working, love," Hildegund said.

Now he did smile. He was proud of his son. Karl was obedient, attentive and hard working. He truly wanted to please his father, and was the best apprentice Fornulf had ever had. Karl would take his mantle as fjorsmythr when Fornulf was gone, and this knowledge pleased him.. Daughters were a comfort, and he loved Berengara, but sons were much more useful.

He took a few coins from the pouch given him by Torgny and gave the rest to Hildegund for safe keeping. Hildegund hugged him goodbye, but Berengara was still scowling as he left the house. Karl had the horses hooked up to their empty wagon and was waiting for his father. Fornulf clambered up onto the front bench with Karl giving him a little push. He was getting too old for wagons, perhaps even for the forge. Under a grey sky, every joint ached and his limbs felt like rusted iron—creaky and stiff.

"You have the bow?" he asked Karl.

"Yes, father," Karl said.

Fornulf nodded. Trolls still roamed the lonely, wind-swept moors in these parts. Men had to be prepared to defend themselves when they left their homes. Every now and then even a great wyrm was said to have been spotted, though Fornulf had never seen one.

Hildegund stood in the doorway and waved to her men as the wagon slowly pulled away along the dirt track. Fornulf glanced back and blew her a kiss.

Two days later, their wagon full of supplies, Fornulf and Karl bumped along the dirt track to their little farmstead in the hills. Their journey had been pleasant and uneventful.

"Mother will be so pleased with the Frankish fabric you bought her, father," Karl said.

"I hope so. It's been long enough since we'd had this much extra silver for any finery. Perhaps your sister will speak to me again after I present her with the silk?"

Karl grinned. "Don't get your hopes up, father. Now, If you'd bought her a nice spear, or maybe a bow, then maybe."

Fornulf chuckled. "True enough."

"Father, look!" Karl said, pointing in the distance toward their farm. "Smoke!"

Fornulf slapped the reins on the rumps of the two horses and their wagon surged forward, as much as it could under the weight of their full load. Karl snatched the bow from beneath the wagon seat and strung it hastily.

Fornulf had a belly full of snakes as they neared the farm. He spied flames licking the low clouds and smoke billowing from his house and small barns. Many of the buildings had burned down already, indicating that the fire had been burning for hours. He stumbled out of the wagon, falling into the muddy lane. Karl pulled him up and together they ran to the remains of their home's threshold.

Fornulf fell to his knees and sobbed, such as he'd not done since his previous wife and children had been taken by the plague.

"Father!" came Karl's voice again. Fornulf turned to see his son kneeling beside their stone well. He ran to his son. Lying there, bloody, and battered, dress torn top and bottom, was his dearest Hildegund. Once again he fell to his knees, sobbing. He threw his body over hers and whispered, "I'm so sorry, love. So, so sorry." He startled when she opened her eyes. Her face was covered in dirt and soot and caked with dried blood.

She tried to speak, but her lips were broken, her teeth shattered. A clearly mortal wound wept blood from her belly.

"Who did this?" he asked.

"T- Tor- " she began.

"Torgny?" he said shocked.

She batted her eyelids.

"Brynn?" he asked. "Did they take her?"

She shuddered with pain as she shook her head.

"Where is she?" he asked.

A single tear washed the soot and dirt from a track along her cheek and her eyes set like the evening sun.

Fornulf held his beautiful Hilde as she faded, departing her mortal coil.

Fornulf worshipped the old gods, but Hildegund had been a

Christian, as were his children. And so he'd fashioned a cross for her, planting it at the head of her grave which they'd dug on the top of a small hill overlooking the bay. Karl spoke words to help send his mother on her way. The sun was easing into the sea as they paid their final respects.

No more tears flowed from Fornulf's eyes that day. Sorrow yielded to cold rage. His revenge would be like the great icebergs that floated in the fjords in spring—slow and inexorable. He would end Chief Torgny. He swore it to the old gods and the new.

Something caught his eye and Fornulf stared down the hill. A shadow moved against the setting sun. He ambled down the hilland soon enough he could make out a figure—a girl!

"Father?" Berengara asked.

"Bryn!" Fornulf hobbled as quickly as his leg allowed and scooped up his daughter. "Gods above, child. I thought you taken or killed."

She shook her head ruefully, eyes red from crying. She was muddy and pitiful, but whole.

Fornulf caressed her dirty cheeks and stroked her hair.

"When mother saw the men coming," Berengara said, "I guess she had a bad feeling. She told me to run. I didn't understand, but I knew she was serious. I lay on my stomach just over the hill and watched the men. That skinny one, the one called Kraka, he got off his horse first and spoke to mother. I couldn't hear what was said, but then he struck her—really hard. Knocked her to the ground. The other men went into the house and barns. I was afraid, father."

"It's all right, Brynn. You were a good girl to do what your mother told you."

"I went and hid in the cave, but I wasn't sure when to come out." Berengara sobbed as her father held her tight. "I heard her screaming," she managed between sobs.

"I'll avenge her," Karl said, still staring at his mother's fresh grave.

"You will not," Fornulf said evenly. "I've lost enough this day."

"Please, Karl, no!" Berengara pleaded.

Fornulf turned slowly to his son. "Do you not think I grieve the loss of your mother? Would that I could storm in and kill his entire household, then so I would. But I am no warrior, and neither are you."

"I could kill him," Karl said sourly.

"Perhaps. But could you kill all his men as well? For they would surely kill you and I would have lost another member of my family." It saddened Fornulf that his son with such a gentle soul should be driven to such fury. Berengara had always been the child with the warrior's heart, but not Karl.

Karl stormed off, cursing and kicking up chunks of sod. Fornulf understood the boy's fury, and impatience. But he'd lived fifty-one winters. He'd seen men hurry to avenge slain family, only to swiftly join them in the afterlife. No, his revenge would have to be slow, deliberate. He knew his strengths and weaknesses. He was no warrior, nor was Karl—though he might be young and fit. It took years to learn to wield a sword properly —years which Torgny and his men had spent diligently.

Firstly, he needed to understand why Torgny had done this. And to do that, he had to live, which meant leaving the farmstead. Clearly Torgny had been intent on killing him, but hadn't found him at home. But why? Why would he do this? And if Torgny meant to kill him, then surely this was far from over.

There was little of value left after the fire, even the remaining gold he'd received from Torgny had been taken. They salvaged what supplies they could, took what they could carry from the wagon, then made for the mountains. Fornulf wished he had a living sword with him. But all he carried was his trusty spear. A solid weapon, to be sure, but with no special abilities except that which came from regular use of the whetstone. Karl carried an old sword of Fornulf's and a hunting bow.

Fornulf and his two children talked as they trudged up the hill path. "We'll seek refuge until I can divine the reason for Torgny's crime. We'll find some way to avenge your mother," Fornulf said.

"Does it matter why he did it? The bastard murdered her,"

Karl objected.

"Son, if we understand the reason, then perhaps we'll be in a better position to succeed. Do you remember what I taught you about forging?"

Karl nodded silently.

"Good. Then you know it matters *why* the iron hardens. If you know *why*, then you can repeat the process, or change it. The *why* is everything. If you know that, then you have the keys to the kingdom, lad. You must understand the motivation of your enemies."

"You sound like a warrior," Karl said.

"Do you think I was always a smith?"

Karl turned to look at his father with a look of incredulity. "You? A warrior?" Karl grinned.

"You find that so hard to fathom?"

"Father, I mean no offense, but you have always been such a peaceful man. And you were born lame."

Fornulf gave his son a rueful smile. "In fact, I was not born like this."

"But- you told us- " Berengara objected.

"I told you a story, children, because I did not want Karl to run off to the shield-wall and die, as I nearly did."

Karl stopped walking suddenly, looking at his father with disbelief.

Fornulf hiked up his right trouser leg and revealed a long

scar which ran horizontally across his shin. It was almost a full crescent, only sparing the back half of his leg. "I told you this was a mishap of birth. Does that not look suspiciously straight?"

Karl nodded.

"In my first shield wall, when I was but your age, some clever bastard struck beneath my shield and nearly took my leg clean off with a flick of his wrist. My leg hung only by the rearmost skin and flesh, the bone having been cloven neatly in two. I suppose that was my salvation, for it healed, thanks to some old crone wise in the ways of leechcraft. Though, it left me lame for many years, and I still suffer its effects thirty-five years on. Later that year, I heard the story of the man who'd wounded me. They said he wielded an enchanted sword made by a legendary fjorsmythr, the life-forger Ulfberht, which was why with one easy blow he'd nearly taken my leg. The wound left me with a nasty limp thereafter, and the leg was weak, so I could no longer become the warrior I'd hoped. The story planted a peculiar seed in me. I began to marvel at a blade crafted so finely, and of course, I had to find some way to earn my way in the world. So I spent the next four years searching for that smith in the desperate hope of learning that eldritch art."

"Truly?" Karl asked, astonished.

Fornulf nodded. "So yes, I know something of war. Though not overly much, I admit. But I never wanted that for you, Karl. I saw how easily those highborn spent young men's lives likes chunks of hack-silver. No, I knew I could do better for you. And so, in order not to encourage any dreams of heroics, I said I'd been born lame. And kept my shameful battle to myself."

"But, father," Berengara asked, "why would you forge blades like the one that nearly killed you?"

"You should have killed the old bastard," Karl added.

Fornulf shrugged. "I admit, the thought crossed my mind, though only for a moment. No, I realized that men would continue to kill men, whether or not Ulfberht crafted swords. And I was very fortunate, for Ulfberht's apprentice had just died of the fever. So he took me on."

They resumed their climb up the hill.

Berengara snatched the hunting bow from Karl's hands and motioned with her hand for the quiver of arrows. "You know I'm a better shot, Karl."

He scowled. "You think you are." He handed her the quiver and shook his head.

"Where will we go, father?" Berengara asked.

"First, we'll seek sanctuary with an old friend."

Chapter Three

THEY PICKED THEIR WAY UP a craggy mountain, on paths that only a goat should have trodden, but Fornulf had been here before, and knew the safe steps. Finally they arrived in a nock in the mountainside at what appeared to be a pile of rocks, no taller than a man's waist, but from that pile smoke billowed gently upward.

Fornulf called out, "I seek a troll wife. Are there any troll wives around?" His voice echoed off the rocky walls.

No reply came, and he shouted again. Karl looked perplexed, but said nothing.

"I seek a limping smith with no balls. Are there any around?"

came the reply in a deep baritone voice.

Not the voice Fornulf was expecting! He shrank back, throwing arms out to hold Karl and Berengara from straying forward. "Show your self!"

An enormous man, clad in a long mail hauberk and carrying a sword and shield stepped out from behind a pile of rocks. Berengara nocked an arrow on the bow and aimed at the warrior.

"I didn't expect to see you again any time soon, you old devil," the warrior said. "Wife kicked you out of your bed?"

"What?" Fornulf was shocked. He'd not ever seem this man before.

"Take a step toward my father and I'll fill you with arrows!" Berengara said with a snarl.

The warrior spied Karl and cooed. "Ooh, you brought me your handsome son! He is most welcome. Fornulf, you can sleep on the floor. *He* can share my bed." He giggled while Karl's face turned a bright red. The warrior pulled a vial of liquid from his pouch and drank it down. Suddenly the big man faded and a woman remained—the seithkona. "Call me Sibyl," she purred. "Sorry for confusing you, old man. A woman alone in the hills has to learn to scare off any would be visitors." She held up the potion and winked.

"Nice trick." She was actually a comely woman, though older than his Hildegund had been. He noticed his son grinning at Sibyl's brazen offer, now that she looked like a woman. Not too many women around the farm, he knew.

Sibyl stopped smiling when she saw the look of utter grief on Berengara's face. "What has happened?"

That night they sat warm and dry in Sibyl's stone hut as rain lashed the mountain. The seithkona had told Karl to call her *aunty Sibyl*. Fornulf knew that was not her real name, for no spirit walker would ever relinquish such power to another, but he thought it sweet that she doted on the boy, treating him now like a son, and not a potential lover. Not too many men up in the crags either, he mused.

Sibyl made Berengara feel very welcome as well, gifting her a finely woven scarf and admiring her beautiful flaxen tresses. By contrast, Sibyl was a woman of raven dark hair and milky skin. They ate well, and Fornulf felt relief that his children were safe. That tiny comfort was a pearl in a sea of oysters.

As the fire crackled in Sibyl's hearth and all were comforted by a bottle of well brewed mead, they talked and they planned long into the night.

Sibyl and Fornulf sat cross legged on a dirty, white bearskin rug. She held her hide covered drum. "We shall make a journey along the limbs of Yggdrasil. The great world tree will allow us to travel to the homes of other spirit walkers and ask them to inquire with their folk about chief Torgny's plans."

Sibyl produced a small wooden stick with a round ball of leather on one end, and began pounding of the drum rhythmically. "Close you eyes, and relax. Listen to my words and heed my commands."

BOOM, BOOM, BOOM, BOOM, BOOM … and on, and on. She continued the cadence relentlessly, like a rowing master beating time for men pulling the oars, but her's was a never-tiring pace.

In short order Fornulf felt his mind and body drift, he began to sway slightly, and had to consciously steady himself.

The drumming continued … *BOOM, BOOM, BOOM, BOOM, BOOM …*

"Soon," Sibyl said in a whisper, *"you will see a great forest, endless trees, green and lush. Do you see it?"*

BOOM, BOOM, BOOM, BOOM, BOOM, BOOM, BOOM, BOOM …

"Smell the air," she continued, *"take in the musty forest, the pungent mosses, decaying leaves, life, death, the cycle continued."*

BOOM, BOOM, BOOM, BOOM, BOOM, BOOM, BOOM, BOOM …

"We are now standing on a path in the great forest. The many branches form a roof above us, shielding us from Sunna's light. All that we see is a diffuse green light, permeating the air around us. The eldritch glow of nature, of life."

BOOM, BOOM, BOOM, BOOM, BOOM, BOOM, BOOM, BOOM …

Fornulf gasped as he caught the scent. A forest. Trees.

Mosses! He was there. He wanted to shout his excitement! *My gods, I'm here.* He'd worked with spirit walkers before, but only as a conduit to his life forging. He'd never journeyed with them.

The drumming continued, but now, it was a whisper, far away … *boom, boom, boom, boom, boom, boom* …

"Open your eyes, Fornulf. Tell me what you see," Sibyl bid him.

"Gods save us!" Fornulf exclaimed. "I'm on a stone path in an endless forest."

They walked for what seemed hours to Fornulf, and as they went, the forest becoming thicker and darker. The canopy seemed to reach up endlessly, but there was no sky to be seen.

"Sibyl," he asked, "what happens to our bodies while we're here?"

"They are quite safe. We are still sitting in my house, and I am still beating the drum. To your children's eyes, we've not departed. And we'll not be gone long, though it may feel days for us. Time passes differently here between the worlds—sometimes slower, sometimes much faster."

"Where did you learn such things?"

"From another seithkona, like me. When I was a young girl, my family began to notice that I saw things which they did not. They knew I had *the gift*. And few have it. So, my father sent me to apprentice with a great volva named Sybil. She taught me many things before she died. And in her honor, I style myself

Sibyl also. Though I suspect that was not her real name either."
She stopped abruptly. "Here we are. Take my hand" She
proffered a hand to Fornulf who took it gently.

He felt a sudden feeling as if he'd leaped off the house roof,
as he'd done accidentally years before. It was a strange feeling,
but passed quickly. Then they were below the path, in another's
house. Though the interior seemed composed of all silver
outlines and had no substance. Like a painting of smoke. A man's
form could be seen, and he seemed to take notice of them, for
he stood and stared at Sibyl.

"Hello, my dear," the man said in a voice that echoed.

"Greetings, you handsome old devil!" Sibyl said.

"Flattery will get you *everywhere*," he said with grin.

"You mean *it* still works?" she asked, eyebrows askance,
finger pointing to his lower regions.

"Cheeky, girl. I assume you must need something? If you
came to flirt you wouldn't have brought a friend, now would
you?"

"I do. We do," she added.

The spectral figure bowed, sweeping an arm across his torso.
"I am yours to command."

"You know of chief Torgny?" Sibyl asked him.

"Balding? Little would-be king of Aegisheim? Yes, I know
him. Treacherous bastard. Had his brother poisoned, the
previous chief, then pushed his nephew off his lands. Bad

business."

"That sounds like him. He's struck again. Only now he's done harm to a friend of mine."

The silvery outline of the man nodded toward Fornulf.

"Yes, he is my friend. His name is Fornulf and he's a good man. A fair man who has treated me well when others have shunned me. I would consider it a favor to me if you were to help him."

"If I can, I will."

Sibyl nodded. "We need to know why Torgny has done this. He ordered Fornulf's house burned and had his wife killed. We assume he was there to kill the whole family, but Fornulf and his son were away, and his daughter hid. Can you help me spread the word through the four farthings, and help to ensure we are warned of any further actions Torgny might be taking? And if any of our neighbors have similar grievances with Torgny and will stand with us, we would know that as well."

"It will be done. And, Fornulf, I'm sorry to hear of the loss of your wife. I too have suffered such as loss."

Fornulf didn't know what to say. He didn't even know to whom he was speaking—or to what. "Thank you. Sadly, this is the second time for me." Fornulf wasn't sure why he'd mentioned that, but he felt he should.

Fornulf's eyes fluttered as he felt weight return to his physical body in a tingling sensation spreading from his toes and fingers to the core of his body. An image of Sibyl's house began to coalesce in his eyes and mind, the scents of her collection of herbs and potions infusing his lungs. He stretched out and caught sight of Berengara's hopeful face.

"Are you alive father?" Berengara asked.

His throat was dry, so he nodded instead of speaking. The ever present pain in his leg assured him that he was indeed alive. Sibyl got up to fetch mead, which she offered to him. He took a sip and felt the warm liquid rejuvenate him.

"Thank you."

"Father," Berengara said, "your beard!"

"What about it?"

"It's longer. Much longer."

Fornulf ran his fingers through his silvery beard. It was.

"I told you, old man," Sibyl said, "times passes differently there."

"There's much I don't know about magic," he said.

"Just how many kinds of magic are there?" Karl asked.

"If you don't count my secret potions and healing herbs, only four," Sibyl said. "The first three are very rare. Two you know of. Your father is a fjorsmythr, a life-forger. He deals with life magic to forge great weapons and armor. I am a seithkona, a spirit walker, who deals with spirits and spirit walking. There are only two more. The vitkur commune with the gods and other worlds to harness the power of the elements: fire, earth, air, and water. Vitkur are very dangerous. The last type of magic is more common, and many can learn, though it takes a lifetime to master —that of the wyrdskapar—wyrd shaper. They have the power to see time, to peer into the web of wyrd, and can read your past, present, and possible futures through the use of the runes. Though, be wary, your future is your own, what they see may not always come to pass."

"Can you learn more than one kind?" Berengara asked.

Sibyl tilted her head from side to side. "Not really. A witch, like myself, might also learn to read the web of wyrd—which in fact I have. But I have never heard of anyone learning more than one of the first three types of magic." She glanced to Fornulf who was shaking his head.

"Nor have I," he said.

"Can you read the runes for me?" Berengara said excitedly. "Will I become a great shield-maiden?"

Karl laughed and Fornulf tried waving him to silence, but he might as well have tried to throw whale oil in the forge to stanch the flames. Berengara was nothing if not mercurial, and scowled at her brother for his scorn. Had they been born noble, she surely would have demanded a place in the war-host so she could make her name as a shield-maiden. But they were common folk, and common folk needed their girls to work.

"Not tonight, sweet girl. It is your father's wyrd that must be read. He has plans to make. For him, I will cast the runes."

Berengara pouted for a moment, but it passed, as did all her girlish moods.

They gathered around the hearth while Sibyl retrieved a small leather pouch. She pulled out a crumpled, white linen cloth, an arm's length to a side, and smoothed it out on the dirt floor.

"When I begin," Sibyl said, "you must envision the question you have for the Norns, the weavers of our wyrd. Only you will understand the full meaning behind the symbols. I will tell you what they represent, but you must puzzle out their meanings in the fabric of your own life. Do you understand, old man?"

Fornulf nodded.

"Then close your eyes and reach into the bag. Draw nine tiles."

Fornulf gathered up nine tiles, cradling them in his cupped hands.

"Now, toss them gently onto the casting cloth," she said, pointing to the white linen she'd laid on the floor.

Fornulf took a very deep breath. He was nervous. Mentally, he asked the Norns to tell him about this summer, and the outcome of his conflict with Torgny. He cast the runes.

Each of the tiles was the size of a small stone, but were fashioned from wood. They had a warm honeyed look to them, with a runic symbol carved on each, stained red.

"Ah," Sibyl said. "See how some gather at the center of the cloth, while others are at the edges? The ones at the center are the seed of your problem, the ones at the edge are where your wyrd may lead you. The runes which are overlapping are complimentary."

He recognized the symbols and had a basic idea of what they meant. He saw Hagalaz, the rune of hail, as Torgny had requested on his sword.

"You see this rune?" Sibyl asked, pointing.

"Of course. It means hail."

"Yes, and more. To a man's future it can mean a disruptive change. You see how it's overlapped with Fehu?"

He nodded.

"Fehu means wealth, such as cattle, gold. It can indicate prosperity."

That made perfect sense to Fornulf. The root of his current problem was another man's lust for wealth and power. Combine that with Hagalaz, and he had a lust for power imposing a disruptive change on his life.

"Down the cloth we have Kenaz, which signifies fire and knowledge. It is close to Jera, which means harvest. It can mean a harvest of crops, or the culmination of hard work. Here, fire or knowledge will lead to a harvest of some kind."

What in the frozen oceans did that mean?

"Next," Sibyl continued, "we have Pertho, which means birth or chance. It is overlapping with two other runes: Ansuz, which means gods or divinity, and Algiz, which means protection."

Now Fornulf wished he'd studied rune reading. "There's a chance I might get divine protection?" he wondered aloud.

Sibyl shrugged. "Perhaps. You'll have to think on that for some time. Lastly," she said, pointing to rune tiles on the farthest edge of the cloth, "we have Mannaz and Isa. Mannaz means man, and Isa is ice."

Fornulf smiled grimly. A frozen man. Perhaps that was to be his end? Alone in the frozen wastes.

"That's all I can tell you, good smith."

"I wish the gods and Norns spoke plainly."

Sibyl looked offended. "Then how would I spend my days?" A slow smile crept over her face, lighting up her eyes. She was beautiful when she smiled.

Chapter Four

ONLY TWO DAYS HAD PASSED before Sibyl was contacted by her fellow spirit walker. She and Fornulf were out walking on a mountain path to take some air when she felt a presence contacting her. She had to sit silently for a moment, eyes closed. When she opened her eyes she spoke to Fornulf. "Do you remember a woman named Idelle?"

Fornulf cleared his throat. He remembered. She'd been the Welsh slave girl he'd bedded one drunken night at the old chieftain's hall. "I- maybe."

Sibyl smirked. Oh Gods, she knew.

"When she heard what happened to you, she helped to

divine Torgny's plans by asking other servants. Brave girl. I wonder why she'd risk so much for you?"

He shook his head slowly, feigning ignorance. That was a good question. Why would she risk Torgny's wrath for a man who'd bedded her once and then never looked at her again? She'd been a lovely girl, but Fornulf had been drowning in guilt once he'd sobered up, and made a point of never being alone with again, or even close to her.

"It seems our chieftain has larger ambitions," Sibyl continued. "According to Idelle and her sources inside his household, Torgny wanted you dead so that you'd never forge another living sword, such as his Isbrunna. He intends to consolidate power here, as the King did in the old country."

Fornulf was burning with fury, and was at the same time drenched with the coldest sorrow. Had he known of Torgny's concern, he could have moved, or agreed not to forge such a blade here again. It was doubtful any other man on the island could afford one anyway. "For nothing," he mumbled, dropping to his knees.

Sibyl lay a hand on his shoulder. "He's also put bounties on your's and your son's heads. Oh, and there's more. Idelle also told us of a plot to poison the last chief that Torgny forced her to participate in. He threatened to murder her son if she didn't."

Fornulf stood.

"What will you do?" Sibyl asked, compassion softening her

words.

Fornulf stood tall before the small hearth in Sibyl's cottage. "It seems our chieftain wants to take all the lands for himself," he told Karl and Berengara. "And I have unwittingly handed him the tool to do just that. I must stop him."

"Father! No, please," Berengara pleaded. "Let us leave this place. Can we not sail to Frankia? Mother had family there."

"I cannot, daughter. Though *you* must. I have too long turned an eye to the evil my work has done, telling myself, that if not me, then someone else would make these weapons. I told myself a convincing lie so that I could earn glory as a smith and sleep with a clear conscience. No more. My self deceit has cost your mother's life. It ends here. I know of no other life forger. I will be the last. But not because Torgny wants it, because I must. Though before I retire from this mortal world, I will make sure his sword is destroyed, and that he pays for taking your mother's life. I swear this to you, and to all the holy powers." Fornulf threw his arms out wide and looked up. "Do you hear me gods? I, Fornulf, son of Harald, son of Ragnar so swear it!"

Fornulf lay on the floor in front of Sibyl's hearth, hand behind his head staring up at the ceiling. Berengara and Sibyl sat huddled in a corner, talking about whatever it is women talked about, he supposed.

Fornulf's plan was simple. He would forge a new living sword, and find a champion to wield to it. His champion would kill Torgny, Fornulf would destroy the sword, and they would all live in peace and prosperity. There were a few problems with his plan.

Firstly, Torgny would be guarding his forge, like as not. But Fornulf had built a second smaller forge, a secret known only to him. He'd never been sure why he'd built it, he simply felt that there might be a need for it someday. Perhaps the Norns were guiding him, even then?

Secondly, who would dare think to kill Torgny? There were surely many who disliked the chief, but he was wealthy and had men to protect him. Any who might try to kill Torgny would need to be paid a fortune, which Fornulf did not have. Or that champion would have to be mad. Sadly, the latter option seemed to be the only avenue available.

Of course, Karl had volunteered to kill Torgny. Fornulf admired his willingness to sacrifice, however misguided, but Karl did not have a warrior's heart or soul. He was simply a young man consumed with grief—such was often a deadly combination. No, he would need a trained warrior—one who stood a good chance of killing Torgny, and with a living sword, an even better one. And he needed that same man to be a bit mad, or to have a very good reason to want to kill Torgny. And if such a man existed, why would he not have done so already? All good questions. And as the days passed, he found answers to them all.

Torgny's nephew, Gunnar, was to be the keystone of this

magnificent arch. He surely wanted his uncle gone so he could reclaim his father's lands. And the young man was a seasoned warrior, having gone raiding to the far eastern part of the world. Some said he'd even been to The Great City herself, Miklagard. And it just so happened that Gunnar had recently arrived back on the shores of the island. Apparently he was back to visit his widowed mother who still lived on her father's farm, far from Aegisheim. That was good news for Fornulf, as it meant Gunnar was far enough away from Torgny as to be safe for a short while.

If Fornulf could get to Gunnar and persuade him to his plan, or rather, convince him that the time was ripe for reclaiming his own lands, then he might have a chance to honor Hildegund. Though in truth, he knew he was satisfying his own honor. Hildegund, being the good and decent God-fearing women she had been, would not have countenanced vengeance. He thanked the gods he hadn't converted to the new faith, as his soul thirsted for retribution.

There was still the matter of a sword. To forge such a weapon he needed a willing sacrifice. He might be able to have Karl finish the forging process. Then he could offer his own life force to the blade. Yes, he would be willing to do that. But did Karl have the skill to master the process yet?

He was getting ahead of himself. He didn't even have the materials to make the sword—he'd need much gold and silver. He still had some diamond dust and sky iron. How could he hope to obtain the equivalent wealth that only one man on the island possessed?

His contemplation was interrupted by shouts for help—Karl!

Fornulf bolted from Sibyl's cottage. The moon was waning , but still lit up the mountainside. And under that silvery light stood an adult mountain troll.

Karl was trying to keep the creature at bay with a sword. The troll seemed to be toying with him, feigning a claw strike, pulling back and laughing.

Berengara and Sibyl burst from the cottage, Berengara with bow in hand.

"Stay back!" Fornulf shouted. "Sibyl, my spear!" Sibyl ducked back inside.

Berengara pulled out her belt knife, holding it against an arrow head covered in pitch and charred cloth. She produced a chunk of flint and struck several times against the steel of the knife until the pitch erupted in flame. She nocked the arrow and loosed—all before Fornulf could warn against it.

Her flaming arrow struck the troll's left shoulder, embedding itself in its flesh, burning the creature. It howled its pain, a sound that turned Fornulf's blood to ice-water in his veins. The creature snapped the shaft off, leaving the arrow head buried. Instead of hurting or even scaring the troll, the wound had infuriated it. And now Fornulf had no spear to hold back the beast as it barreled over Karl, knocking his son down, and charged at Berengara.

There was no thought to Fornulf's action. There was only danger and his child. His body was the only shield he could provide her. He gave it willingly, knocking her aside and throwing himself into the path of the troll. The impact was like being run over by a charging warhorse, he mused, as the creature slammed into his body. He heard the sounds of breaking bones—his, not the troll's, then the pain hit him.

Berengara did not hesitate when he'd pushed her aside. By the time Fornulf had fallen, she'd lit and shot another flaming arrow, this time into the troll's back, as it had pivoted when it collided with him. Fornulf saw it turn back to his daughter, a glint of inhuman evil in its eye. It was not the dispassionate look of a wolf killing a sheep, for the wolf took no pleasure in killing the sheep, only in the nourishment it provided. This troll enjoyed the hunt, the kill.

Karl had recovered by this time and hacked down at the troll's back as it moved toward Berengara again. The troll spun, and Berengara loosed a third flaming arrow, again in its back where it couldn't reach. The creature's flesh was aflame now, crackling like roast pork. It roared, and Fornulf winced. Once again the beast turned back to Berengara.

Suddenly there was a flash of moonlight and Fornulf could see flame glittering off a spear head. Sibyl thrust Fornulf's spear deep into the troll's belly. At the same time Karl hacked at its neck with his sword and Berengara loosed two more flaming arrows.

Berengara stood triumphantly over the burning corpse of the troll.

"You're a stupid girl, Brynn!" Karl shouted at her.

She scowled at him. "You yelled for help."

Karl was clearly flummoxed. "I was yelling for father, not my little sister. You could have been killed."

"I saved you didn't I? How about some gratitude?" She shook her head in disgust and tromped off.

Sibyl leaned over Fornulf, binding his broken bones and making him drink foul tasting potions. "You're a stupid old man. You know that?" she said. "*You* could have been killed."

He made to laugh, but moving at all was terribly painful. "You too?"

"She's quite the little shield-maiden," Sibyl said smiling, gesturing with her chin toward where Berengara had walked off.

"Such have always been her dreams. Though her mother and I did try to dutifully dissuade her. She never took to naal binding."

Sibyl laughed. "Nor did I."

"How badly am I wounded?"

"No cuts, just three broken bones. Your left arm has two breaks, one upper and one lower. And you have one broken rib.

Count yourself lucky, old man. That troll could have had you for lunch—literally. Had you daughter not had those troll-arrows ready," she trailed off.

"The old gods tell us, when you walk out your door, have your weapon close at hand. I didn't think Brynn paid attention to my silly stories."

"You're lucky she did."

He nodded. Yes, he was lucky he had two brave children. Though, he was unlucky that he had broken his arm—he needed to forge a new living sword in a few weeks. Would his bones be healed by then? He doubted it.

Sibyl sent out a call to all her fellow seithkonas. They were to spread the word to a handful of trusted men about Torgny's plans to grab power, and asked to contribute gold and silver for the forging of a new sprit sword. Some even offered their men and swords to the cause.

In less than a week, they had all they needed. The materials had been delivered to a safe location where Sibyl retrieved them. Fornulf was shocked at the outpouring of support. Apparently he'd underestimated how poorly folk thought of Torgny.

Now all he needed was a champion.

Chapter Five

THE FOUR TRAVELLED WEST BY night, walking under the cloak of darkness, and in the shadow of the jagged central mountains. A two day journey was made five by the necessity for stealth. In the western fjords lay the home of Gunnar's mother's people, and Fornulf hoped, his champion.

They arrived at the end of the fifth day, with the sun descending into the sea. Barking dogs heralded their arrival and stooped figures oozed out of the low turf houses that were cut into the ground.

They approached the largest house, which Fornulf hoped was the village tavern.

"Who goes there?" an old man asked.

"It is Fornulf, the smith. I come seeking Gunnar, son of Niall."

Fornulf sensed trepidation from the old man. Like as not, he'd heard about the bounty Torgny had put on them.

"Do ya, now? Seems men are looking for you too, smith."

"Aye, they are. The same men that stole Gunnar's rightful lands, and murdered his father."

The old man gaped for a moment, then ushered them inside.

Before they had a chance to enter, a man came barreling headfirst out of the tavern. He rolled into a heap on the ground. Three burly men followed the first out. They shouted and cursed the man on the ground kicking at him.

Fornulf did what any civilized man would do, he intervened, though carefully. His left arm and ribs were still tightly bound.

"Hold!"

"Piss off, old man! Unless you want to join this filthy dog on the ground," one of them said.

"Filthy dog?" said the man on the ground. "Your sister didn't seem to think so." Fornulf could smell the drink on the man from several yards.

That earned the man a kick, but he must have been ready for it, as he grabbed the attacker's leg and rolled into it, knocking the attacker flat onto his back. He rolled right over him and was up on his feet, grinning.

The other two men drew their swords, and the defender drew his with a smile.

"I told you, your sister came to my bed willingly," he said, "that's no crime on this island. If you have issue with her behavior, then by all means, discuss it with her."

"Oh, we'll discuss it with you, Gunnar."

Gunnar? This was his champion? A maiden defiling drunkard? Gods above.

The first man got to his feet and also drew his sword. He thrust in at Gunnar, who slipped to the side and slammed the flat of his blade onto the back of the first man's head, knocking him senseless. "Walk away," Gunnar said, "or someone is going to get hurt!"

"Yeah, you!" said the second man as he hacked down at Gunnar's shoulder. Gunnar spun toward him, parrying the blade and elbowing the man in the jaw, causing him to stumble to his knees.

The third man thrust at Gunnar's exposed back when he'd turned to parry, but Gunnar was ready. He flicked the blade of his sword up and took the man's ear off with a neat stroke.

The last man fell to his knees, clutching the bleeding ruin at the side of his head. Thoroughly defeated, the first man helped his comrades up, then they hobbled away from Gunnar, cursing and shooting foul looks in his direction.

Gunnar sheathed his sword and shook his head. "I didn't

want any trouble."

"Might have thought of that before you bedded that one`s sister," Fornulf said.

Gunnar affected an indignant look. "Of course I did. But you should have seen their sister! A roll in the cattle byre with her was worth it." He gave a hearty laugh and made his way back into the tavern.

Inside, it was cramped but cosy. A central hearth kept the tavern warm and provided a focal point for guests. Low beds arrayed along the walls doubled as benches during the day. At night men could pay for beds to sleep.

Under the dim torchlight of the tavern, Fornulf finally took the measure of Gunnar. He wore a plain white tunic, now soiled with mud. A luxurious mane of light-brown hair cascaded over his shoulders. His beard was neatly trimmed. A handsome young man by any account.

"May I buy you a drink" Fornulf asked.

Gunnar nodded. "There's quite a bounty on your head, old man." He jerked his chin at Karl and Berengara. "And for them. Though, I might keep the girl for myself. She's a pretty thing."

Fornulf knew the insults were bravado, and part of any young warrior's repertoire. He'd spread such himself, thick as manure on a spring field.

"I believe I may be able to offer you something of much greater worth, Gunnar."

"Not likely. You'll be caught or dead soon. What can you offer me?"

Two women greeted the rest of Fornulf's party kindly and had seated them, offering mead and beer. Hospitality was almost a religion in the frozen wastes.

"Would you like to return to Aegisheim?" Fornulf asked. He could see immediately that he'd hit a nerve as Gunnar's face grew red enough that he could see the change even in the dim light.

"It's not called Aegisheim," he said in a low rumble. "It's called Frithgard. That puddle of weasel piss, Torgny, renamed our lands after he stole them."

"Your uncle?" Fornulf prompted, taking a seat beside Gunnar on a bench.

The man nodded grimly.

"There's something you might not know about your father's death." He let that hang for a moment and could see Gunnar was intrigued. "His death was not of nature or chance. Torgny poisoned him."

Gunnar's eyes bore into Fornulf now. "Have you proof of this?"

"None that we can use at the Quarter Court or the Althing, but proof enough to know he did it. A slave administered the poison on his behalf, and of course she cannot testify against her master."

"Are you certain?"

Fornulf nodded. "I know the slave personally. And I have several well landed men who'll back my tale."

"That nithing!" Gunnar cursed. A nithing was a curse reserved for oath-breakers and the abusers of small children.

"I mean to see your uncle pay for what he did to me and mine. Will you help me?" Fornulf asked. He leaned in toward Gunnar and whispered, "I can give you the power to destroy him and seize back your lands and titles."

Gunnar had left the tavern to retrieve his supplies, leaving Fornulf with his children and Sibyl. As the four sat in the tavern, Fornulf explained his plan. Karl was furious.

"You want me to finish a new sword, then kill you? My own father? You're mad!"

"Karl, it's the only way. Gunnar will fight Torgny, but I must arm him. Even the finest blade would be no match for Isbrunna. You know the power in those swords."

Karl's temper seemed to subside. "I want to avenge mother, and make sure that piece of filth doesn't hunt us, but I'll not kill my father to do it. What do you think mother would say to such a plan?"

Fornulf exhaled. He knew all too well what Hildegund would have said. "Karl, we must. Even if we leave this island we will not be safe, Torgny will hunt us. Not just to prevent me from forging another living sword, but to salve his pride. He can't allow us to just slip away. Not if he plans to consolidate power. That would make him look weak in front of the other chieftains."

Karl shook his head and walked out of the tavern. "I'll have no part in this."

Sibyl was close by and put hand on Fornulf's shoulder. "He'll come around. Not to worry, old friend."

Her subtle floral scent stirred something in him. Fornulf wanted to embrace Sibyl. That was something he treasured here on the island—abundant natural hot-springs meant its folk bathed regularly. Continental folk were terribly malodorous. Had Hildegund ever worn such a scent? Living near the vapors he'd never have been able to tell. Their home was suffused with the acrid smoke, and the smell of rotting eggs.

He yearned for a soft embrace more than anything. He was so weary. Would that he could hold his dear Hildegund one last time.

Sibyl offered a wan smile mixed with a look of sorrow, as if sharing his pain.

Berengara sidled up to Sibyl. "Sibyl, may I speak with you?" She cleared her throat. "About … a woman's matter?"

"Ah," Fornulf muttered, "I'll take my leave." He kissed his daughter's forehead and scurried away, allowing them their privacy, and in truth, escaping before he heard anything he didn't want to. He hadn't considered that his daughter was now motherless. Gods, what did she need to know before he married her off? He shook his head, not wanting to think about such womanly things. He'd hire an old woman to advise her. Yes, he'd do that.

As he left the tavern, he saw Sibyl hand Berengara a vial— probably a potion to ease the pain of womanhood? So many things he didn't understand.

With Karl gone for a while, Fornulf was free to consider his options more deeply. Sibyl suggested that they could buy a sacrifice for the living blade with some of the gold gifted by the other chiefs. It would be a stretch, but the overly generous donations were enough. Some slave's son would give his life to free his family. Though Fornulf did not relish taking a life, he knew that it was a noble gift and respected that. Many young men spent their lives much more cheaply.

When Fornulf had sent her away, Berengara had fought like a cornered wolf, only leaving in a storm of fists and nails. He'd sent her to the coast where a ship would take her to the continent. There, she would travel to her mother's relatives. Fornulf needed to know she was safe. He could ill afford any distraction.

The weeks passed all too swiftly as the moon waxed full, and thanks to Sibyl's potions, his bones had mended well.

As stealthily as they could, Fornulf, Karl and Sibyl travelled to Fornulf's secret life-forge, carrying the materials he needed. Gunnar was to meet them there with the sacrifice.

The second forge was small. Similarly constructed on the

side of one of the smoking mountains, and fully functional, it would give them what they needed. They got to work quickly, shaping the block of rare metal that would become the blade and instrument of their vengeance.

They worked hard. As the evening faded, the formless hunk of iron, chunks of hack silver, and nuggets of gold, speckled with diamond powder, grew into the vessel of a future living sword. Fornulf quenched the steel in whale oil and nodded to Gunnar, who left the forge.

He came back with a naked boy.

This boy did not tremble, nor did he wear a look of fear. Did he understand what was about to happen? The boy smiled at him. That unnerved Fornulf. Had they drugged him? If they had, the sword would not accept him. His sacrifice had to be voluntary, and not coerced or cajoled in any way.

Fornulf could not smile back. He helped the boy onto the stout oak table where he lay down.

"Do you offer your life force willingly to the sword?" Fornulf asked.

"I offer my life force willingly to the sword," he said.

"You must hold the blade against your body," Fornulf said.

"I know, father." And he held the blade along the length of his chest and abdomen.

Father? Had the boy just called him father? His mind raced. No, he was simply tired and confused. And he had an island to save and his wife to avenge, this was no time for distraction.

Sibyl and the vitki entered the forge solemnly and began their chanting and drumming. Fornulf held the boy's head gently, stroking his hair, offering some comfort to the poor lad who was about to die. Soon the boy's body began to fade.

"Goodbye," he whispered.

Fornulf's hand wavered. But he could not, he must not falter. Fornulf had a heartbeat to act, or lose the sacrifice. He drew his knife across the boy's throat, blood spurting into his eyes. He gasped as the physical body faded and only the sword blade remained.

He picked up the blade tenderly and put an ear to the steel. He heard it whisper—heard *him* whisper. *"Hevner, I am called. The avenger."*

Fornulf finished the hilt and handle of the sword during the night, and in the morning he presented it to Gunnar.

"Hevner, she is called—the avenger."

Gunnar's face was slack as he held the sword tentatively. Fornulf knew the young man had never seen a sword so fine, let alone held or possessed one.

"You see the runes on the hilt of the blade?"

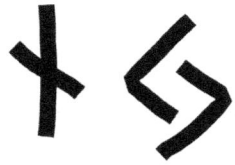

Gunnar nodded. "The first is called Nauthiz, the rune of need. It can heal you. The second is called Jera, or harvest. It will reap vengeance on those who have wronged us."

"Thank you, Fornulf," Gunnar said, still marveling at the sword. He ran his finger along the central groove. "I see small circles, like the pattern of a mail hauberk?"

Fornulf nodded. "Aye, each sword is unique. Their patterns are like the marks on your palm. One is never like another."

Gunnar was grinning. "I can feel the power of it, and hear its voice!"

"She will talk to you. They all do that. And you can to her."

"Why do you call it a she, when it was a boy's life which the sword drank?"

"Women give life, create life. When a new sword is birthed our tradition has been to honor our wives and mothers. The living swords become she."

A slight tremor in the ground alerted Fornulf. Then, growing slowly louder, a low thunder echoed off the canyon walls. Fornulf glanced up to the sky, but saw no lightning. The sound grew louder and more clear. Not thunder—hoofbeats. Hundreds of them.

"Torgny's men!" Gunnar shouted.

Fornulf felt his limbs go cold. There was no time to escape. He snatched a spear and shield from the walls of his forge and Karl did likewise. He spun to Sibyl and the vitki. "Go! Hide!"

"I will not run," the old man said. "I will stand with you."

"You're a fool, vitki," Fornulf chided, but he was secretly glad to have the old sorcerer with him.

"Sibyl, please? You know what the men will do to you," Fornulf pleaded. He'd grown fond of her and wanted to see her safe as well.

She snarled, pulling two daggers from beneath her tunic. "What about what I'll do to them? I'll cut their balls off and feed them to the trolls." She grinned mischievously.

Must he lose all the women he cared for? What had he done to offend the gods? If he survived this, he vowed to make great sacrifices to atone for whatever ill he'd done them.

Two old men, a woman, and a boy—that was sum total of the force which would have to repel a host of Torgny's warriors. "If we die tonight, then at least we shall feast in Valhalla!" Fornulf said.

As the galloping herd of horses came into view under the moonlight, Fornulf noted grimly that he'd been right. There were hundreds. They would die this night. The best they could hope for was a quick death, but from what he'd heard of Torgny recently, that was quite unlikely.

Karl hadn't wavered, and Fornulf marveled at his son's steadfastness. The boy had never fought—not even against another child. Though, Berengara had. Karl was a good natured lad, always had been, and it was bittersweet for Fornulf to see the flames rising again in his son's heart.

"Don't let yourself be captured!" Fornulf warned. "Kill as many of them as you can. Let them pay a high price for their treachery!"

Fornulf, Karl and Gunnar formed a three-man shield wall, with Sibyl and the vitki behind them. Fornulf could hear the vitki chanting now. Was he working some galdr spell?

As the horses came within a bowshot, the vitki's chanting broke like wave against the cliffs and a bright light burst from his wand, burning off the last moonlit shadows. The horses reared and men threw arms up, covering their face, but all were blinded. The light remained, like the sun suddenly risen, its full fury aimed at the riding army.

"Attack!" Fornulf shouted, and they marched forward, spears ready.

"Fornulf!" one of the riders shouted. "You damned fool! We're here to help you. Hold, I say!"

"That sounds like my cousin," Gunnar said.

"Gunnar, is that you? Tel that crazy old smith to snuff out that damned light. By the gods, I think he's blinded me."

"Vitki," Fornulf shouted back at the sorcerer.

The vitki slumped to his knees, clearly spent. Such magic took a toll on the caster's body. The light faded but it took a moment for all of them to see again under the moonlight.

They were not Torgny's men. None of their shields bore the

Aegisheim symbol.

Fornulf approached cautiously as the lead rider, a mountain of a man with long golden hair, slid from his horse, still blinking and rubbing his eyes.

"Damned wizards," the man muttered.

"Fornulf, this is my cousin, Iarnbjorn," Gunnar said. "On my mother's side," he added.

Fornulf remained confused. What were these men doing here? "Why are you here?"

Iarnbjorn's face turned sour. "Why are we here?" he turned to Gunnar. "Does he have all his wits about him?" He tapped a finger to his temple.

"Of course I have all my wits about me!" Fornulf snapped.

"We are here, old man, because *you* sent out a call. *You* named Torgny a usurper. *You* asked for support. We sent you gold and silver. Now we send you men and horses. Shall I go home? I have two pretty slave girls warming my bed—I promise you, I'd much rather be in their embrace that in this foul smelling canyon of yours."

Fornulf laughed.

"He *is* mad," Iarnbjorn said.

Chapter Six

THE NEXT MORNING, UNDER THE ever present iron grey skies, over two-hundred riders began the two-day journey west to Aegisheim, in the South farthing. They represented eight of the thirteen districts within the four farthings. That meant that a majority of the island's leadership supported Fornulf and Gunnar's cause against Torgny.

Fornulf caught sight of a shadow moving swiftly along the top of the canyon wall. A man perhaps? Surely Torgny didn't have spies this far from Aegisheim? A goat like as not.

He turned his mind back to their new army. They might have waited for more men to rally, but could not take the chance

Torgny would learn of their plan. Of course, Aegisheim was already well defended, but Torgny could further reinforce the place, had he advance knowledge of the coming attack. For now, they had the advantage of surprise, and eight gothis—chiefs— rode to confront the would-be usurper of the thirteen districts. He might have stolen Aegisheim from his nephew, but he'd have a much tougher time taking the others.

On the first day's march, scouts had put the run to a hill troll, enticed down by the smell of the horses and men. One troll was no match for a group of well armed warriors on horseback. Trolls preferred easier prey. Otherwise, their journey was uneventful and spirits were high.

Late on the second afternoon, they approached a hill, over which, lay Aegisheim. Now was the time to marshal their courage and prepare to attack.

"How will we attack the fort, father?" Karl asked.

Fornulf took a deep breath. "I believe Gunnar plans to form a shield wall and attack the gates. It's not subtle, but it has the merit of being simple."

"If I were defending, I'd just pepper the attackers with arrows. They'll all be killed." Karl protested.

Sibyl, who rode beside Fornulf, smiled at Karl.

Fornulf nodded, appreciating his son's ability to see the flaw in a plan. "Quite so. Though, this shield wall will be different. The first row will present their shields like you might expect, creating a dense vertical shield-wall. Now, the back rows, they'll hold shields over their heads. This creates a shield in all directions. Making them invulnerable to arrows and spears. We call it the dragon's back."

Karl beamed as he nodded.

"Our archers will shoot at the defenders on the wall to try to give the dragon's back time to breach the gate," Gunnar said. "The biggest men will wield their two-handed axes and chew at the wooden gate. It takes time, but it's the simplest method. Had we more men, and time, we could starve them out. Once the gate is down, our horsemen will ride in and take Aegisheim."

"It sounds easy."

Fornulf shook his head gravely. "It is anything but easy. Simple, yes. Easy? Far from it. Men will die today, son. And it won't be a quick peaceful death like those sacrificed at the fjor'tyna. Men here will scream and cry, as wounds turn them from brave warriors to babes calling for their mothers. I've seen it before."

"I thought Torgny had only fifty men there? Surely with such overwhelming numbers we'll win easily?"

"Walls count for many men. I've heard of twenty holding back a thousand," Fornulf said.

"I'm beginning to dislike your plan, father."

Fornulf chuckled grimly. "The realities of warfare." He shrugged. "Which … is why I became a smith."

Gunnar and his uncle's warriors were ready to move out. "Wish me luck, old man!" Gunnar said.

"What? You're going to be in the Vanguard?" Fornulf asked.

"If we win this battle, men have to have seen me lead. If we win and I'm safe in the back, then I'll earn no honor, no glory. If we lose ..." he tossed up his hands and laughed.

Iarnbjorn reined his horse in to stop beside Fornulf.

Fornulf knew Gunnar was right. But he also knew it was a huge risk. It was all in the hands of the Norns now. "You have my wishes and my prayers, Gunnar." Gods above, he needed this man to win the day.

Gunnar led twenty-five shield warriors, marching in step toward Aegisheim's gate, the cadence of their footfalls rhythmic. Three axe wielders were protected in the center, like the meat of a nut.

Fornulf nurtured a modest, but growing sense of confidence. Though, until the gate was down and the town seized, the battle was like casting the runes—some wyrd was involved, some luck, and a measure of skill.

The remainder of the riders walked their horses down the hill, just out of bowshot of the fort's walls, but close enough to rush in once the gate came down.

A few of Torgny's warriors, manning the wooden parapets, began to shout curses at the approaching formation of shields and men. A few tried their luck with bows, but the arrows bounced harmlessly off the dragon's back. Good, as they should.

"It's working!" Karl cheered.

Now at the gate, the front rank of shields parted so the axe men could do their work. He saw great arcs of steel flashing in late afternoon sun. Their progress warmed his heart—until he saw a large group of men pop up along the palisade all at once—Torgny among them. The bastard was holding up Isbrunna, as if to taunt Fornulf.

Torgny made a downward slicing motion in the air with Isbrunna, as if he were chopping something. Archers began loosing flaming arrows all around the attackers at the gate.

The ground itself burst into flames, engulfing the dragons' back in a conflagration. It was if the dragon itself were breathing fire. Gunnar and the men screamed and howled, making sounds Fornulf had never heard, nor ever wished to hear again.

One of Torgny's archers shot one man who was burning, mercifully killing him. Torgny struck the man with the pommel of Isbrunna and threw him over the wall.

"Let them burn!" Torgny shouted, staring at Fornulf.

"How?" Iarnbjorn asked Fornulf, but he had no answer to give.

Fornulf shook his head.

Iarnbjorn's archers moved forward and began shooting, putting down their own men ... and their chief's nephew, Gunnar. Fornulf's champion was dead.

"Bastard!" Iarnbjorn shouted. "We'll have to retreat."

Fornulf didn't have time to argue. Behind the riders, more flaming arrows carved bright arcs in the darkening sky. Fire erupted behind them, tracing a ring around the remaining army. They were trapped.

Fornulf looked up to the heavens. "Why?" he muttered. Torgny and his man Kraka, rode out the edge of the ring of fire, Torgny's white stallion skittish near the smoke and flames. Because he held a green leaved branch, he'd come to treat, and Fornulf and Iarnbjorn were honor bound to give him safe passage. Bows were lowered.

The bastard had done something, since the flames were still burning, hot and wide. He must have filled a trench of gravel with oil or pitch. And he must have been warned.

Torgny got his horse under control by a cruel application of reins and bit. He sneered at them. "So, my neighbors come to visit? Swords in hand? Tsk, tsk, tsk. How rude." His smile faded and he shouted, "and what have I done to you? You treacherous sons of whores! I should let my men burn you all. You deserve no more."

Iarnbjorn and the remaining six chiefs with Fornulf said nothing. Torgny wasn't here to negotiate a surrender, he'd come to dictate terms. Fornulf waited for the hammer blow.

"Fornulf, my old friend!" Torgny said, as if he truly meant it. "Why have you rallied these men against me?" He looked hurt.

"You know why." Fornulf had no desire to play games with

this snake.

"You wound me. I was saddened to hear of your wife's passing. Hildegund, she was called, no?" The corners of his mouth turned up into a cruel smile.

Fornulf's temper would have been boiling—had he been a younger man—but he was an old man, and he knew the word-tricks others used to shake a man's calm. They were every bit as dangerous as a sword blow and should be dodged and blocked just the same. Strength wanes but wisdom waxes, he mused. How sad the two couldn't coexist in equal measure. What great men could then be forged.

"Nithing!" Karl shouted.

"Boy, keep silent!" Fornulf chided his son. He did not want this situation exacerbated. They were no longer in the strong position. Their only chance was cunning. He had to out think this greedy creature.

Torgny's face went slack, and as if sensing his cold fury, his horse skittered sideways, receiving a firm slap for its trouble.

"Nithing? Me? You dare challenge me boy?"

"I dare!" Karl roared.

Fornulf grabbed Karl's shoulder, but the boy was much stronger and shrugged him off. "Come and fight me, coward! Or do you only attack women alone in their homes? You have no honor, Torgny. You call yourself chief? Chief of what? Chief of lies and deceit, I say. Oath breaker!"

Torgny slid from his horse. "I am going to skin you alive, little boy. Very, very slowly. I'll hear your cries like the sweetest song. Like the one your mother sang." Torgny laughed. He turned to his rake-thin henchman. "Isn't that so, Kraka?"

"Oh, yes, Lord!" Kraka said enthusiastically.

Fornulf was amazed that Karl held his temper in check, but he felt his son's fury turn from an inferno to that of a cold roiling sea. Karl moved forward and Fornulf tried to stop him. He held up a hand. "Father, I must do this."

Fornulf protested, but his son would not listen.

"Father, Torgny will surely kill us whatever happens. Better for me to duel Torgny and die by the sword rather than be burned alive or possibly crucified."

It left Fornulf's stomach feeling like a barrel of eels, but he knew his son was right.

"I, Karl, son of Fornulf challenge you to holmgang for the slaying of my mother!"

"I did no such thing!" Torgny cried.

"You want to play word games? Very well. You ordered, or caused to have her murdered. Is that better?"

"I admit nothing."

Karl shook his head. "And, you ordered, or caused to have your brother poisoned. Then you took Gunnar's rightful lands and kicked him out. Do you deny that?"

Torgny wore a contemptuous sneer. "I have your great army

surrounded by fire, and with a word, can have you all killed. I have no need to deny, object, or otherwise even treat with stupid creatures like you and the rabble behind you." He jerked his head at the other seven chiefs, who of course could hear the whole bitter exchange.

Fornulf was curious now, for as he'd watched Karl challenge Torgny, the seven chiefs had been huddled together, whispering. Now Iarnbjorn stepped forward.

"What if we were to offer you something, Torgny," Iarnbjorn asked him.

"And what could you possibly offer me?"

"You want to be over-chieftain of the island? Is that not so?"

Torgny didn't respond.

"Let us speak openly, Torgny. Good men have died today. I would that no more should perish. Let me assume that what I said *does* represent your goal. If that were so, then even if you kill us here today, you would still have to fight our kin. We didn't empty the dales to march here today. Many more warriors remain to defend what's ours."

"I'm listening," Torgny said.

"What if we eight were to bend the knee to you. Offer you our support should any other chiefs not bend the knee willingly. Surely that would make your consolidation of power easier, cheaper, and much faster? We here are all land owners. When our tenants die, rents go unpaid, sheep scatter, and fish stop filling our nets. It's hard on a man's hoard when such times come. Would you be willing to consider such an offer?"

"If my goals were as you said, then I might. But of course such an offer must come with a cost?"

Iarnbjorn shook his head. "No, not really. Well, a minor thing for a man such as yourself." He let that statement hang, and Fornulf could see Torgny getting antsy. Surely he could taste victory as if he already had his tongue in the honeycomb.

"Well, what minor thing?" Torgny demanded.

"There is a matter of honor that we feel must be settled. There has been an accusation that you murdered Gunnar's father, your own brother. And there is a witness to this. You know, as well as I, that there is no weregild that you can pay for the crime of killing a member of your own family. But you can atone for the murder of Fornulf's wife. There is but one price. If you enter the ring of hazel with Fornulf's son Karl and settle this by holmgang—a duel to the death—then we will follow you. And ... you let him wield Gunnar's sword."

"Ha!" Torgny balked.

"He'll never agree to it," Fornulf whispered to Sibyl.

Sibyl leaned in close to Fornulf's ear and said, *"I might be able to change his mind."*

Fornulf watched as Sibyl sat down, cross legged amidst the warriors. With eyes closed and a look of pure serenity on her face, she began to beat her drum.

"What fools," Torgny muttered to Kraka. "I have them surrounded by fire. And I have this," he said, thrusting Isbrunna toward Kraka. "Why would I risk a duel with that foolish boy?"

'For honor' came a whispered response.

"Who said that?" Torgny spun around, livid. Not a man on the wall stirred, nor were they close enough to whisper. He turned to Kraka and scowled. "What did you say to me?"

Kraka looked horrified, as he should have. "I said nothing, Lord."

Torgny turned back to his enemies trapped inside his ring of fire. It had been a brilliant plan, suggested by a Byzantine monk visiting his house. They'd dug a ring shaped pit, filled it with gravel, then soaked it in a special mixture of rather nasty oils and powders. They topped that with a thin layer of soil, and the trap was set. Those Byzantines were a nasty lot.

'Coward.' The voice whispered again.

It could only be Kraka. He was the only man near to him. Torgny slammed Isbrunna's hilt into the side of Kraka's head, knocking the mouthy bastard on his arse. "Next comment that leaves you tongue, I'll skewer you!" He spat on Kraka's still form and turned his attention once again to his enemies.

'Fight the boy, or live in shame, coward.'

Torgny spun on Kraka, ready to impale the man, but Kraka was unconscious. He prodded the man with his foot. Nothing.

'Fight Karl Fornulfsson, or you will be forever cursed. Doomed to hear

me whisper in your ear till Ragnarok come.'

"Silence!" he screamed. The line of enemies were staring at him now. He felt his temper beginning to boil. The one thing Torgny hated above all else, was appearing the fool. Which was why he worked so hard to know more than everyone around him. Perhaps he should fight this boy? Put the whole mess behind him?

'Yes, you should fight him. You must fight him. Coward.'

Where was the voice coming from? Was it only in his head? He'd heard of men going mad. Surely this would not just happen in one instant?

"What say you, Torgny?" Thorkill shouted at him firm across the wall of flame.

'Do it. Do it. Do it. Fight him, kill him, regain your honor. Coward. Nithing!'

"Stop it!" Torgny bellowed, grabbing his head. They were all staring at him now. Curse them all.

'Fool. Stupid little boy. Useless. Good for nothing. Pissed your pants didn't you?'

How? There was only one person that had ever said such things to him. "Father?" he whispered?

'Killed your own brother! My son, and now my grandson. Fight, or I will drive you mad. You useless, shameful little cur.'

Torgny was on the edge of tears now, trembling, Isbrunna becoming harder to keep hold of.

"Of course I'll kill the little bastard!" Torgny bellowed, with confidence that rested only on his tongue.

"Lord?" Kraka croaked, coming to.

Torgny said nothing, but buried Isbrunna's blade deep into Kraka's stomach as he tried to sit up. He felt a chilling wind flow across his arms and through the sword.

"Isbrunna," he whispered, and shivered.

Chapter Seven

TORGNY HAD SOMEWHERE FOUND HIS own vitki, a man closer to dead than alive, but with a cunning glint in his eyes. The old sorcerer cast a spell to lower the flames for a moment, over which Torgny allowed three to pass: Fornulf, Karl, and Iarnbjorn. The rest of the warriors remained confined in the ring of fire.

Fornulf hadn't liked the idea, but they were lucky for any opportunity at all. Thank the gods Sibyl had been able to make contact with Isbrunna's soul in the spirit world, and convince it to help influence Torgny. Fornulf had no idea such a thing was even possible—the implications for other living swords were terrible. What havoc a seithkona could wreak, if she chose.

Worries for another day. If Karl lost, Torgny would surely have Fornulf put to death, but he'd no longer care. At least Berengara was safe—hopefully now in the warm embrace of her mother's family. His name might not live on, but at least a small part of him might.

Torgny's men brought Gunnar's sword and armor for Karl to use. The armor was stuck to Gunnar's melted skin and Fornulf saw Karl wincing with disgust at the foul odors of burnt flesh and shit. Gunnar's helmet came off more easily.

Torgny's men had laid out a ring of hazel boughs, ten yards across. There Fornulf's and his son's fates would be decided.

Each man was allowed two shields, which were round, made of linden and came with a heavy iron boss. Karl strode into the ring, appearing proud and fearless. He and Torgny were of similar builds, neither giants, but both fit, and muscular. Torgny had apparently been a warrior in his prime, though he was slightly passed it now. Each of them wore a fine coat of mail. Torgny's shone more brightly, for he had slaves to polish it with sand, and Karl's was burnt and covered in chunks of flesh—but it would keep him safe.

Both wore conical helms with a long nose bridge, though Torgny had armor around the eye as well. Fornulf had seen neither of them fight, but he prayed that youth and vigor would win the day here. It often did. Karl had played with Fornulf's swords, but had never received any real training.

The local Lawspeaker had been summoned to guarantee that the holmgang was fought honorably and to declare the winner. He asked them if they both accepted the terms of the duel— they did. When Karl drew his living sword, Hevner, for the first time, Torgny realized he'd been tricked. He expected an easy victory with his own living sword in hand. Isbrunna would surely have prevailed against a common weapon. Now the odds were slightly more even. Fornulf saw the fury flash across his face. Torgny couldn't back out now. He'd just agreed to the terms and accepted the Lawgiver's judgement. His fury passed and Torgny smiled.

"You sneaky old, bastard," he said to Fornulf.

With a drop of the Lawgiver's hand, the duel began.

Torgny banged his sword hilt against his shield, like a drum. It was something men did in the shield-wall to feed their courage. Karl made no such show. Instead, he lunged, thrusting his shield out as Torgny's blade lay flat against his shield. Karl trapped Torgny's blade against his own shield and swung Hevner in an arc, back around Torgny's head. Hevner rang Torgny's helmet like a bell as it glanced off. Torgny thrust Karl away with his shield and shook his head.

Fornulf was encouraged. First strike went to Karl. No blood, but that must have shaken the old snake's confidence. Fornulf felt a surge of elation. Maybe his son would prevail!

The opponents circled each other, as rams often did before they butted heads. The duelists clashed in much the same way. And like two rams, they collided. Sword slammed into shield, rang off helmet, struck armor. And so it went.

Fornulf had to admit, Torgny was a decent warrior. Too bad he was a terrible man. A kind man in that body, and with that wealth, could make this island a much better place to live. But such were the dreams of simple men like Fornulf, not of thieves like Torgny.

Karl hammered Torgny's shield, shattering it like a thin sheet of ice. But then he stepped back, allowing Torgny to fetch his replacement. Such were the rules of a holmgang.

For a moment Fornulf thought he heard drumming again. Perhaps just echoes in his ears from the swords and armor clashing.

Torgny's speed and endurance appeared to be waning. Though after receiving his new shield, he struck first. Instead of slamming the iron boss of his shield at Karl, he held the shield flat, thrusting the edge at Karls' shield. This had the effect of pushing Karl's shield flat as well, exposing his neck and shoulder to Torgny's sword. Torgny must have put his very soul into that swing, as Isbrunna hacked through Karl's mail armor and cut deep into his shoulder.

Karl stumbled back, wincing. His shield arm dropped and Fornulf spied blood seeping through his mail. Gods, Torgny must have cut him deeply. And he knew it too. For the bastard smiled, suddenly looking more energetic. Had he been faking the fatigue? Deliberately slowing down to trick Karl?

Blood was clearly streaming from Karl's shield arm now. He'd have to finish Torgny quickly if he had any hopes of winning. A few minutes bleeding like that and he'd be dead, or at best, too weak to stand.

Torgny exploded forward with a lunge. It would skewer Karl, as he couldn't seem to lift his shield high enough now to block it. What Karl did next was brilliant, and maybe just lucky. He pivoted at the waist, allowing Isbrunna to skim over his armor. As Torgny rushed by, Karl left a foot out, tripping Torgny. The snake was down. Karl thrust down for the killing blow, but Torgny rolled, thrusting Isbrunna up into Karl's mail, piercing it, and sending the blade so far through, that the tip could be seen protruding from Karl's back.

Torgny stood, Isbrunna still buried in Karl's guts. He stood face to face with Karl and smiled as Fornulf watched the life fade from his son's eyes.

His son ... gone. It was over. They had lost. Fornulf felt nothing. Bereft of enough emotion even to cry.

"No!" Karl screamed, eyes wide. He managed to yank up Hevner and impale Torgny through the guts as well.

Torgny snarled, gasping, as he pulled Isbrunna from Karl's stomach, gore dripping off the blade. Karl knelt, still holding

Hevner inside Torgny. Torgny dropped his shield and grabbed
Isbrunna's tip with his shield hand, holding the sword across his
body in two hands, then slammed the flat of Isbrunna's blade
onto edge of Hevner, shattering Karl's sword.

Torgny spat into Karl's face as the boy fell back dead. Torgny
fell to his knees, blood bubbling from his mouth, and he laughed.
"I- kkrrgh- I won."

As Fornulf watched, wanting to weep, he heard a sound like
wind hissing through a small crack in the door. It grew louder
and higher pitched as Torgny sputtered and tried to stand,
Isbrunna still in hand.

A black mist rose off the ground, hovering within the ring
of hazel. It came from Karl's body. No. It came from Hevner! It
hovered over the bodies like a varthir—a wraith. Then it impaled
Torgny like a spear, penetrating his body, suffusing him. Torgny
screamed in agony, arms outstretched.

Then a silver mist coalesced around Isbrunna, which Torgny
still held. It too, struck Torgny like a spear, and seemed to drive
out the black mist, which once again haunted the hazel ring. A
great flash of shadow blinded Fornulf.

As he rubbed his eyes, dark blotches clouded his vision. For
a moment he thought he saw a creature with wings. He closed his
eyes and opened them. A woman with black wings, an ornate
helmet, clad in mail, and carrying a great war spear, floated above
the hazel ring.

"My gods," he whispered. "Brynn?"

The Valkyrie smiled. "Yes, father." It was Berengara, he was sure of it, but she sounded like a woman now, not like his little girl.

"How? What happened?"

"Don't you remember? We said goodbye already."

"What?"

"When you forged Hevner."

"No," he whispered.

Berengara nodded.

"I had to."

"But how is that possible? There was a boy on the table. I saw him. I touched him."

She gave him a sad smile and he knew she felt his loss. "A friend of ours helped me. When you sent me away… " she shook her helmeted head. "I couldn't go. I knew that was not my wyrd. You remember when Sibyl read the runes for you?"

He nodded weakly.

"The fire and harvest. That was your future. Your spark cultivated this harvest. It led to Torgny's downfall. Three of the runes were for me; the rune of the gods, of protection, and of birth. They created me as a protector. I am a valkyrie, chooser of the slain. I am called Brynnhilde now. Brynn, for the name you lovingly gave me, which means armor. And Hilde, for my dear mother. Together it means Hilde's Armor. And so I am."

Fornulf was almost dazed at this revelation. He wanted to weep, to be sad, but how could he be? His daughter was not dead —not at all. She was a valkyrie. A tear ran down his cheek, but not from sadness. Then it occurred to him that his daughter was —or had been—a Christian. "But, how can you have become valkyrie? They are part of my old heathen gods?"

She smiled with the mischievous look he was so used to. "Oh father, I just let mother believe that. I didn't want her to be disappointed in me, as you were for me being less than ladylike."

He wanted to say she was wrong, that he hadn't been disappointed. But that would have been a lie, and this was no time for deceit. Fornulf's heart was breaking for a third time in two months. He swallowed hard. "Your mother would be proud."

"She *is*," Brynnhilde said smiling.

"So am I," he said, and meant it with all his heart. "You always wanted to be a warrior Always playing with my spear and sword." He shook his head in amazement. A coughing noise startled him and he saw Torgny rise up.

Fornulf grabbed at his belt knife, ready to plunge it into the back of the snake's neck. By the gods, he would not rise!

"Hold!" Brynnhilde's command shook the ground beneath her father's feet. That was no mere word! Gods above! Fornulf froze.

Brynnhilde floated to the ground and approached her father. She picked up Isbrunna, which Torgny had dropped finally. She whispered to Fornulf, *"Torgny is not dead."*

"But I must kill him!" her father protested.

"Worry not, father. Nor is he in his body. You'll find my brother Karl alive and well, inside the body of this older man. I have already explained this to Karl. He is still confused, but will get past it." She pointed to Torgny. "Trust me. Trust him. He's a good man. And with your help, he'll be an even better chief."

She handed Isbrunna to her father and whispered one last thing, *"Take care of this sword. As long as Isbrunna is whole, Torgny's life force will remain trapped within. Let him remain there till Ragnarok. And may it be the last sword of its kind."*

He nodded. "I'll see it done."

Once Torgny had been defeated, Karl/Torgny had his vitki suppress the ring of fire and the trapped warriors had been allowed to go free.

Sibyl ran to Fornulf and threw her arms around him, kissing him. That shocked him. And pleased him.

"I thought you were about to die, old man," she chided.

"I might have a few years in me yet, witch."

Karl/Torgny ambled over to Fornulf and the Lawspeaker, who stood near. "I- um- I am going to forgo my previous claim. Despite the outcome of the holmgang, I believe … I may have been mistaken. Yes. I was mistaken to try to seize my neighbors land. Let us forget this ever happened."

The Lawspeaker was clearly flummoxed at Torgny's change

of heart and his rambling.

The eight chiefs who heard Torgny, cursed at him, but seemed happy enough not to have to bend the knee. Freedom would reign on the island once again.

Karl/Torgny bent close to Fornulf and whispered. *"How did I do?"*

"You need practice. You're not a very good Torgny."

"Thank the gods," Karl/Torgny whispered.

"What now, Lord?" Fornulf asked his son, more formally.

"We feast, of course, smith!" Karl/Torgny grinned.

Fornulf turned to the seithkona and held out an arm. "Sibyl, will you join me?"

She seemed to scowl for a moment then leaned in and whispered, *"Only if you call me Anna."* She winked and took his arm.

Thus ended the reign of chief Torgny. A sad story, I know, for it is mine. That foul valkyrie creature also told her father about the last two runes; the ones for man, and ice—the man was me, and the ice, well, I think you can puzzle that out.

And so, here I lie, in the Metropolitan Museum of Antiquities—trapped inside Isbrunna—my eternal prison. Of course I've hoped, nay, prayed, that Isbrunna would have rusted and crumbled, releasing me from this prison, but that tricksy bastard, Fornulf, he'd considered that. If you'll notice the plaque —yes, that one. The little bronze thing.

* * *

On permanent loan: courtesy of the Jonathan H. Fornulfsson Foundation

Fornulf's son, Karl, created a living trust which is administered to care for the sword. That trust makes a permanent loan of Isbrunna to various museums. They all take such good care of me—curse them all! Oh, I almost escaped during the last great war when I was on loan and the city was blitzed, but some clever fool rescued me, returning me to my this lovingly crafted display case.

I hate you, Fornulf! Do you hear me!

Of course, he didn't.

ALSO BY HUGH B. LONG

The Yggdrasil Codex: Book 0

Star Wolves - The Tribes of Yggdrasil: Book 1

Star Fury - The Tribes of Yggdrasil: Book 2

Star Viking - The Tribes of Yggdrasil: Book 3

ABOUT THE AUTHOR

HUGH B. Long is an Award Winning Canadian Journalist and Best Selling Author. He writes full time, and is passionate about Science Fiction and Fantasy rooted in Viking Mythology. He also writes Norse and Viking themed non-fiction under the pen name – Eoghan Odinsson.

Graduating from the University of Aberdeen's School of Engineering in Scotland with his Masters of Science degree, he subsequently taught for the University, and was a dissertation advisor for graduate students.

In addition to his academic background, Hugh also holds a Black Belt in Shito-Ryu Karate, a Brown Belt in Budoshin Ju-Jitsu, and was study group leader in D.C. for the Association of Renaissance Martial Arts. (Historical European Martial Arts). Hugh has taught Martial Arts in Canada and the USA.

Hugh recently returned from a 10 year stretch working in the Washington D.C. area, and is now back in his native Ottawa Valley where he lives with his wife, son and two dogs.

For more information:
Website: www.hughblong.com
eMail: author@hughblong.com
Twitter: @hughblong
Facebook: HughBLong.Author